MR. MISCHIEF

by Roger Hargreaves

Poor Mr Happy had had a tiring day.

Rushing here and there and back again cheering people up was hard work.

"Phew," he sighed, as he went into his house and sat down for a well-earned rest on a kitchen chair.

But then, do you know what happened?

It fell to bits!

BUMP, went poor Mr Happy.

"That's all I need," he said. "I rather think that I have had a visit from Mr Mischief."

He was right!

Outside Mr Happy's house, and running away as fast as his little legs would carry him, was a small mischievous figure.

Mr Mischief!

"Oh mischief, glorious mischief," he cried. "I do so love it!"

And he ran, giggling, into the night.

The next morning there was a knock at Mr Greedy's front door, but when he went to answer it, there was no one there.

But, what was there was a box.

And, inside the box, was a large chocolate cake filled with cream and with the most delicious-looking pink icing.

Mr Greedy's eyes gleamed.

He licked his lips, and shut his eyes, and opened his mouth, and took a large bite.

UGH!

The chocolate wasn't chocolate.

It was mud!

The cream inside wasn't cream.

It was cotton wool!!

And that delicious-looking pink icing wasn't icing at all.

It was toothpaste!!!

And, outside Mr Greedy's house, and running away as fast as his little legs would carry him, was a small mischievous figure.

Giggling as he ran.

That's not all.

That very same morning, Mr Funny discovered that someone had filled his hat with treacle.

Very sticky treacle!

Can you guess who that someone might have been?

However, that very same afternoon, Mr Mischief did something that he was to regret.

He was walking along through the woods, looking for mischief, when he came across a wizard.

A fast asleep wizard.

"I know," giggled Mr Mischief, "I'll change the wizard's wand for an ordinary piece of wood and then he can't do any magic."

He grinned a mischievous grin, and crept quietly towards the slumbering wizard.

Mr Mischief reached carefully out and seized the wizard's magic wand.

But what he didn't know was that wizards' wands don't like to be seized.

"HELP!" shrieked the wand in a high shrill voice, and awakened the wizard, who in turn seized Mr Mischief by his nose.

Which was extremely painful!

"Led go ob by node!" cried Mr Mischief.

"I know who you are," said the wizard. "You're that Mr Mischief who sawed through poor Mr Happy's chair legs, and," he continued, "baked a rather unusual cake for poor Mr Greedy, and," he went on, "put treacle in poor Mr Funny's hat! I've been hearing all about you," he added.

"Led go ob by node," cried Mr Mischief again.

"Very well," said the wizard. "But don't believe that you can get away with being as mischievous as that!"

And, as he let go of Mr Mischief's nose, he got hold of his magic wand, and waved it.

"Beware," he said, and went off.

"Silly wizard," muttered Mr Mischief. "Can't you take a joke?"

And he went home.

"Silly wizard," he said again, as he sat down in his kitchen.

BUMP!

"Silly silly silly wizard," groaned Mr Mischief, picking himself up. "Him and his silly magic!"

And he made himself some porridge for tea.

"Mmmm," smiled Mr Mischief, as he put a large spoonful of porridge into his mouth.

"AARGH!"

Somehow, as if by magic (which of course it was), the porridge had turned into . . . sawdust!

"Oh dear," spluttered Mr Mischief. "Perhaps I had better not get up to quite so much mischief in future after all."

And he went upstairs.

He jumped into bed.

SPLOSH!

The bed was full of raspberry jam.

Ugh!

"Oh dear, oh dear," sighed Mr Mischief. "I think I definitely must not get up to quite so much mischief in future!"

And do you know something?

The day after he was as good as gold.

And the next day.

And the day after that.

It lasted a week!

And then, that old mischievous urge got the better of him.

He just couldn't help himself.

It was a Saturday night.

He crept into Mr Fussy's house when he was fast asleep, and can you guess what he did?

"Oh, what a beautiful piece of perfect mischief," he cried, as he ran giggling home.

He'd cut off half Mr Fussy's moustache!!

Isn't that terrible?

Poor poor Mr Fussy.

He was absolutely horrified when he awoke and found out.

But even that terrible piece of mischief is not the end of Mr Mischief's story.

So . . .

. . . before you read this last page, just take a look out of the window.

Go on!

You can't see a small mischievous figure anywhere about.

Can you?

Are you sure?